# LOSS TO INSANITY

## ANOTHER JULIA LILLUS CRIME THRILLER

## JAMES ROBERTS

Edited by

### JAMES ROBERTS

Illustrated by

### JAMES ROBERTS

Cover Design Copyright © 2020 James Roberts

Cover Art Copyright © 20120 James Roberts

Illustrations Copyright © 2019 James Roberts

ISBN: 978-1-7361234-5-4

Library of Congress Control Number: 2020923087

Published by James Roberts Publishing

Printed in the United States of America

This book is a work of fiction. Names, characters, businesses, places, events, and incidents are either the products of the author's imagination or used in a fictitious manner. Any resemblance to actual persons, living or dead, or actual events is purely coincidental.

❀ Created with Vellum

# CONTENTS

# INTRODUCTION

This book is a work of fiction and continues with the other Julia Lillus Series of Crime Thrillers by James Roberts.

"A husband loses his wife; a father loses his daughter. He devises a warped method of having his daughter return to him; only the path he takes results in unheard-of methods, murder, and utter horror."

# VIETNAM

Somewhere in the jungle.

---

"Hey, this is Lieutenant Ronald Tier. Where the hell is air backup? We are getting heavy fire from the 'Cong'; we can't move!"

"Sir, we are on our way. I suggest you take cover and start backing your squad away from the jungle. We will soon be laying down Napalm."

"It can't come soon enough! These 'gooks' have us penned in, and we won't be able to hold them back much longer," says Ronald.

"We will be there, momentarily. Just hold on!"

"Yeah, sure. What do you want me to hold onto...my dick?" Ronald mumbles to himself.

---

"Hey, Ron, I see your tour over here is over after next week."

"Yeah, I won't miss this God-forsaken hell hole!" exclaims Ronald.

"Come on! You know you will miss the 'boom-boom girls' with

their tight pussies. But, put it this way, they probably gave you a going-away present you will have for life. You never know what those pussies are infected with over here."

"Why don't you just shut up, Tom! You know the whole time I was over here, I only fucked one of them."

"Yeah, that sixteen-year-old who doesn't get out to walk much because she is always on her back with her legs spread, or did you keep her on her hands and knees?"

"Tom shut the fuck up!"

"Just saying. That little Asian hottie wasn't only fucking you."

# BACK AT HOME

T he officer's wives are patiently waiting at the bus-stop, waiting for them to arrive.

---

"Lilly, when is your Ron supposed to arrive today?"

"He said the bus should arrive around one o'clock today. I can't wait to see him!" exclaims Lilly.

"My Johnny is supposed to arrive at about the same time. Maybe they are on the same bus," says Sally.

"I haven't seen Ron in over a year. He was home for a month when they sent him home due to the wound he got from sniper fire, and then they sent him right back," says Lilly.

"This war we are in is menacing. Why is the United States sticking their nose in Vietnam, anyway?" asks Sally.

"I don't know. I just want my Ron back safe and sound. He has a baby to be happy about," says Lilly.

"Oh yes. When are you due?"

"I am at eight months. Ron hasn't seen me showing. After all, I conceived when he was home for that short period," answers Lilly.

"I guess you guys got right to it as soon as he came home."

"You better believe it! Months without sex is unbearable, at least for me," says Lilly.

"Well, if it weren't for my 'little tickler fella,' I wouldn't survive myself," says Sally.

"Yes, I know what you mean. Fingers and bananas work very well, too."

"You got that right, Lilly."

---

"Oh my gosh, Lilly, look at you…and that baby bump!"

"Oh, Ron, I couldn't wait for your return. I was hoping you were going to be out before our little bundle of joy is born."

"Lilly, I wouldn't miss it for a minute."

"Ron, we have so much to catch up. Tell me, how was it over there?"

"Lilly, I don't want to talk about it. It is a real mess over there, and that is all I want to say."

"OK, darling, I will fill you in on what has been going on here. Betsy down the street had twin boys. They are so adorable, and Lucy, Ted's wife, had a baby girl."

"Well, I can see others in this neighborhood were just as busy as we were. Speaking of that, you think we can get some more of that?" asks Ron.

"I don't know, Ron. Eight months pregnant and with this bump, I am not sure how."

"How about we put some pillows under the baby bump while you straddle them on your hands and knees?"

"Oh, you mean you want to enter 'doggy' style?"

"Exactly! Let's go to the bedroom and see how it works out."

"Ron, I have missed you so much! I would do anything to get 'laid' now you are home," says Lilly.

# COMMUNITY BEAUTY PAGEANT

C hief Julia Lillus enters into conversation with Officer Bobbie
Peltz.

"Bobbie, how are the plans coming along for the Community Beauty
Pageant? You know how I feel about them," says Julia.

"The committee said they are all set to go. The Pageant will be next
Saturday," says Bobbie.

"Well, if you are carrying another girl in that baby bump of yours, I
hope you do not plan on entering her in one of those Pageants. I just
think it is wrong to make a little girl look and dress like a teenager. It
all as to do with sex appeal, and that should not be part of a child
growing up. It is bad enough they do it with teenagers. No wonder we
have so many problems with rape and pregnancies. Keep sex out of
their lives until they become adults and respect for what it is. Now,
are you tired of hearing me on my soapbox?" asks Julia.

"You are so right, Julia. I would never enter my daughters into one
of those Pageants. There is no way Richard would allow it even if I
tried," says Bobbie.

"Did you get the files on the registered local and surrounding pedophiles? We need to be on the lookout for them during the Pageant. How about clowns? Do we have any of those showing up?" asks Julia.

"No! We don't need any more incidents with clowns like we just had with Judd Finney," says Bobbie.

# AT THE HOSPITAL

R on and Lilly Tier are in conversation with the doctor.

"Mr. Tier, you can come in and see your wife now."

"Is she all right? What about the baby?"

"There were complications, but your baby daughter is OK and healthy," says the nurse.

"Hi, honey!"

"Ron, come over here and look at your baby daughter. Are you still OK with her name, Samantha?"

"Yes Lilly, Samantha is just fine. The nurse said that there were complications. What did she mean by that?"

"I am not sure, Ron, but I heard the doctor say he didn't think I could carry another baby."

"What! I want a passel of babies!" exclaims Ron.

"Honey, calm down. Let's wait to see what the doctor has to say."

"Mr. and Mrs. Tier, I am Doctor Fine, and I would like to congratulate you on being parents to a beautiful and healthy child."

"Doctor, what were the complications with my wife, Lilly?" asks Ron.

"That is why I am here. Lilly has a discrepancy in her blood, and it caused issues with the pregnancy and the delivery. In laymen's terms, there was a battle going on between Lilly's blood and the baby's."

"But are they OK? What is wrong with her blood?" asks Ron.

"Your baby is just fine. We will do more tests on Lilly to see what is going on."

"Doctor, Lilly said something like she cannot bear more children?"

"Mr. Tier, I strongly suggest it for the time being until we find out what is going on. I wouldn't want to endanger the lives of your wife and baby."

"But doctor, what could be so wrong to cause danger?" asks Lilly.

"Let's wait to see what the results are from the tests. I am sure you are not ready to get pregnant right away, are you?"

"No, doctor, I am not," says Lilly.

# THE PROSTITUTE

Officer Richard Peltz arrives at the Hartford Police Department with a prostitute.

---

"Richard! What do we have here?" asks Julia.

"This girl propositioned me out there on my way back from lunch."

"What? How old are you, missy?" asks Julia.

"I am sixteen and will be seventeen next month."

"Oh, here we go again!" exclaims Bobbie.

"Missy, do you realize prostitution here in Harford and most places is against the law?" asks Julia.

"My pimp didn't tell me that. I am new at this."

"Well, missy, besides me taking you to your parents and getting from you your pimp's name and how we can get a hold of him, you and I are going into that room, and I am going to talk to you about selling your body!" exclaims Julia.

"Uh-oh, Richard. She is in for a rude awakening when Julia starts in with her," says Bobbie.

"Poor girl," says Richard.

"Richard Peltz, what do you mean by that? Were you thinking of taking her up with her proposition?" asks Bobbie.

"Hell, no! I just think it is unfortunate these young girls feel they have to sell themselves, that's all."

"OK, I will buy that," says Bobbie.

# RICHARD AND BOBBIE

The two enter into an intimate game.

---

"Look, I will pay you one hundred dollars if you will show me what is under that blouse and an additional one hundred if you will show me what is under that skirt," says Richard.

"Sounds good to me just to show you my bra and panties," says Bobbie.

"Oh no, that money is to show me what's under those"

"Fine. I can do that, but if you are planning anything else, you will have to pay me another two hundred."

"We will see about that."

"Richard put me down! Where are you taking me? Where is the money?"

"Sorry, I am not paying you anything! You are going to see how I am going to make a 'deposit'!"

"Richard, please be careful. I am pregnant!"

"No problem, at least I won't have to wear a condom."

"It appears you never do anyway," says Bobbie.

"Just lay down here. Enough talk; now, some action."
"Richard, we shouldn't be using the break room for this."
"Julia will be with that prostitute for a while. She won't hear us."
"Richard, dear, you always get your way."
"Yup, now take off those panties!"

# LILLY TIER IS GIVEN BAD NEWS

R on and Lilly Tier are once again facing the doctor and receive devastating news.

---

"Mr. and Mrs. Tier, I have the first round of test results, here, to discuss with you."

"Doctor, is it bad?" asks Ron.

"Well, I am afraid so. It appears that Lilly has a blood cancer to which we call Leukemia."

"Cancer? Oh no, what does that mean? Can it be cured?" asks Lilly.

"We will try all we can do. A bone marrow transplant may extend…."

"Extend what?" asks Ron.

"Extend her life."

"What the hell? She will die with this?" asks Ron.

"I am afraid the answer to that is, yes. I feel Lilly will have two to three years at the very best."

"Oh," Lilly starts to cry.

"Honey, we will beat this. I know we can," says Ron.

"At first, she won't show signs of the disease, but gradually she will develop symptoms and gradually go downhill in her health. I have set up counseling for you two and a complete schedule of outside care to come to your home to administer what is needed to make you comfortable, Lilly."

"What about our daughter? Is this passed down to her?" asks Lilly.

"No, this cancer is not hereditary."

"That damned Agent Orange! I will bet that is what did it. I passed it to you when you conceived," says Ron.

"No, Mr. Tier. You did not give your wife cancer. We are not sure how it develops or why, but it was not transferred to Lilly when she conceived your child."

"What are we going to do?" asks Lilly.

"My suggestion is for you two, and your daughter to take as many vacations as you can, now, and enjoy yourselves in meaningful relationships before the disease takes complete hold of you, Lilly."

"We need to go home and sift this all out," says Ron.

"You do that, and I want to see you, Lilly, back here in a week," says the doctor.

# JULIA TOYS WITH RICHARD AND BOBBIE

While Julia was counseling the prostitute and Richard and Bobbie were playing their 'game', Julia toys with them on what they have been doing.

---

"Bobbie, you look a little disheveled, and you, Richard appear to be a little out of breath," says Julia.

"We were rearranging the furniture in the break room. It sure is a strenuous undertaking. I am all sweat from it," says Bobbie.

"Did you get the couch in the correct position? Oh, and I hope you didn't get any of that 'sweat' on the cushion covers," says Julia chuckling.

"Oh, no, we were very neat and didn't mess up a thing," says Richard.

"You guys! Was I thinking of the word 'horny'? No, I didn't think that at all! A passel of Peltz kids...yup, that is what I was thinking about," says Julia.

# RICHARD IS OFF TO FIND THE PIMP

Julia tells Richard to find the pimp while she devises a plan for the safety of the prostitute.

---

"So, how did your talk with that young hussy go?" asks Richard.

"Well, you must know I laid it on quite thick. I think once I take her to her parents and have a talk, she will think twice about selling herself," says Julia.

"Were you able to get from her the name of her pimp?" asks Bobbie.

"Yes, she had no problem telling me. She is so new on the street that she doesn't know divulging the name of her pimp is dangerous. That is why we are to be with her at all times until we get her pimp," says Julia.

"What is your plan, Julia?" asks Richard.

"Bobbie, I want you to be by her side at all times after I bring her back to the office from my visit with her parents. She does have a day job down there at Shakeys. I will stop by and tell them she will not be working for a couple of days. I am asking you to spend the night, here with her, until we get the pimp apprehended," says Julia.

"No problem, Julia," says Bobbie.

"Richard, I will give you the name of the pimp and where you can find him. Read him his rights and bring him here. Do not let him see the girl, so make sure you radio Bobbie when you are bringing him in," says Julia.

"OK, I am on it!" says Richard.

"Wait a minute! Do you guys need some alone time? After all, Bobbie will be here for a few nights," asks Julia.

"Well, we could……," says Richard.

"Richard, you have had enough! We are good, Julia," says Bobbie.

"OK, you two, I did ask," Julia says with a smirk showing on her face.

# RONALD TIER IS ANGRY

R on places blame for Lilly's cancer.

"Lilly, I am scared. What are we going to do? How do we tell Samantha?" asks Ron.

"Ron, I am scared too. You will have to tell Samantha about me.
When she can understand, I will have passed on," Lilly says as tears
begin to stream down her cheeks.

"Lilly, honey, please do not think that way. We are going to get
through this. I am not ready to give you up. I am back, and we have a
lifetime to live; the three of us," says Ron.

"Oh, sweetheart, I wish it was going to be like that...," says Lilly.

"I am so mad! I am so mad at the whole world! Why you? Why do
they have to take you from me?" asks Ron in anger.

"Honey, you mustn't feel that way. It isn't anyone's fault. It just
happens. It does you no good to be mad at everyone and the whole
world," says Lilly.

"That damn government! They robbed me, sending me over to

that hell hole, and for what? So I could come back and watch my wife die?" asks Ron.

"Ron, you have to calm down! This hatred you have is not good for you and won't change a thing. I am going to die, and that is all there is to it!" exclaims Lilly.

"Oh, honey, I am so confused and sad. Why? Why does it have to be you?" cries Ron as he places his head in Lilly's lap and bawls.

# THE PIMP

R ichard finds the pimp and brings him to the Department.

---

"I assume you have had your rights read to you?" asks Julia.

"Yeah, you cunt! What the hell you got me here for, anyway?"

"Sir, I am arresting you for operating a ring of prostitutes and endangering the welfare of minor females with the intent to sell sex," says Julia.

"You have no proof of that! It is not my fault those sluts want to sell their pussies. It's not my problem. I didn't tell them to do that!"

"Well, sir, we have proof, and it will be up to the courts to decide. Let me warn you, there isn't much of a chance that you will be found innocent when some of those very young girls you used to sell sex on the streets, testify to the fact that you are their pimp," says Julia.

"You are just a cunt cop! Someone needs to shove a corncob up your ass, bitch!"

"Richard, place him in the cell! The officers are coming as we speak to bring him to the County Corrections Facility. I don't want this filth in my Department," says Julia.

"I can smell your crotch bitch! You aren't too old to walk the streets!"

"Listen, buddy, when you get in jail, you will be the one with something shoved up your ass, and you will wish it was a corncob!" exclaims Julia.

"Richard shut the door! We are through with him!" exclaims Julia.

"Julia, you are a tough cop. I don't know how you can put up with all of that. They get real personal, don't they?" asks Richard.

"Hey, at least their comments generally make out that I am a female worth looking at! No, I could give a damn what they say to me. It doesn't bother me a bit. I have experienced worse throughout my life," says Julia.

"Yes, you have, Julia. By the way, you are a female worth looking at," says Richard.

"Richard, take Bobbie home with you tonight. I think you need to recharge. Poor Bobbie!"

# LILLY TIER'S TIME HAS FINALLY COME

R on tells the doctor Lilly's health is much worse.

"Doctor, Lilly seems to start showing symptoms of the disease. She says her joints are starting to hurt, and her appetite is slipping. I try to get her to eat to keep her strength up, but she refuses. She doesn't seem to care so much for Samantha. I play with our daughter most of the time now. What can I do?" asks Ron.

"Mr. Tier, the reason Lilly's joints are hurting is because this type of cancer causes more white blood cells to be made, and it is causing her bones to swell. She will need to start on morphine soon, and we will need to administer drugs to slow the expansion of her bones. You will need to get used to being with Samantha and bringing your daughter up. Lilly is too weak to do that. I am sure she still loves her. You will continue to see Lilly's health fail as time goes on. This type of cancer is very destructive, and watching someone struggle with it is just devastating."

One month later.

---

"Doctor, how is Lilly? She seems to be getting worse, and it has only been a year since the diagnosis," says Ron.

"Mr. Tier, I am afraid Lilly's cancer has taken a turn for the worse and is advancing at a faster rate than I thought."

"What can we do?" asks Ron.

"There isn't much we can do except keep her out of pain as much as we can. The swelling of her bones is excruciating, much more than she already experiences."

"Are you saying Lilly has to have more Morphine?" asks Ron.

"Yes, she will be on a high dose. She will be asleep much of the time. I suggest you have some meaningful conversations with her in the next couple of days before we increase her dosage."

"Doctor, are you telling me I will not be able to talk to her after that? When will I be able to talk to her?" asks Ron.

"Mr. Tier, it is best you say your 'goodbyes' now."

---

A few weeks later.

---

"Hello? The Langer Brothers Funeral home. How may I help you?"

"My name is Ronald Tier. We had spoken about a month ago."

"Oh, yes, Mr. Tier. Is it your wife, Lilly?"

"Yes, it is time. My poor Lilly has left this world," says Ron.

"We will be right over. Have you changed your mind about the service?"

"No, it was Lilly's wish not to have calling hours and to be cremated. Our daughter shouldn't see her mom in the condition she is in," says Ron.

"OK, Mr. Tier, we will be over within the hour."

# JULIA THE BABYSITTER

A few years have gone by since Lilly Tier's passing.

"Bobbie, you and Richard have been very busy with your little darlings. Why don't you bring them over to my place? I am sure Jessica, Janice and little Julia Ann will have fun playing with Nicole's daughter. Besides, I want to play 'mother' for a little while," says Julia.

"That sounds like a great idea, Julia. I will bring them over right after I am finished here," says Bobbie.

"Richard, you and I have the afternoon off. Julia is taking all three of our darling girls this afternoon. What would you.......?" Bobbie stops her immediate conversation.

"Well..," says Richard.

"Yes, honey, I agree. Let's have a nice dinner and relax in front of the television until we are tired enough to fall asleep," says Bobbie.

"Bobbie, dear, I have to make a slight revision to our plans."

"Oh, no, here it comes," says Bobbie.

"Yes, a nice dinner is fine; relaxing in front of the television is fine, but heavy petting will start until we fall into bed and make love!" exclaims Richard.

"Sorry, honey, I have a slight revision. We don't fall into bed; we 'ride the rollercoaster' right here on the couch!"

"Sounds like a plan, you sexy vixen! Let's skip dinner and get right to it. The first one to get their clothes...off... That is just not fair, Bobbie! How can you get your clothes off so fast?"

"Maybe I want to 'ride the rollercoaster' first!"

# SAMANTHA TIER

**M**uch time has passed, and Samantha Tier has grown into a young middle schooler. Ron has done well, bringing up Samantha, but his anger grows daily.

---

"Daddy, why do you have so little patience with me?" asks Samantha.

"I am sorry, honey. I am just mad at the world for taking mommy from us," says Ron.

"But daddy, you have been like this for a long time. Mommy left us some time ago. Don't you think you should stop being so mad at everyone?" asks Samantha.

"That damned war; they took her from us. It isn't fair!"

"How is that, daddy? There was no war when mommy left us," says Samantha.

"You wouldn't understand. I just hate the world and the people in it," says Ronald.

# THE LOSS

Unrelated and on the other side of town from Ronald Tier's home.

---

"Myla, are you going to the party this weekend?" asks Wanda Sneer, Myla's mother.

"Yes, I am, and Tom is going along with me," says Myla.

"I am not fond of Tom going with you. He has been a bit of a distraction to you lately."

"Oh, mother, he is just a friend."

"A friend? Since when do 'just friends' kiss frequently?"

"I can't help it if he kisses me."

"Look, Myla, I don't want Tom driving you to the party."

"No, mother, I will be the driver. We have been over this many times before."

---

Back at the Tier residence, Samantha, too, will be going to a party.

---

"Samantha, whose house did you say the party is happening?" asks Ron.

"It is at Cindy's house a couple of blocks away," answers Samantha.

"Would you like me to drive you over to Cindy's house?"

"No, daddy, I can walk. It isn't too far, and there are some friendly dogs on the way I would like to pet."

"OK, be careful and stay on the sidewalks."

"I will, daddy. Please don't worry. I am a big girl, you know," says Samantha.

"You are all I have, sweetheart!"

---

The weekend of the parties has arrived. Samantha is finishing up getting dressed and ready to go to Cindy's house, and Myla is waiting for Tom to arrive.

"Tom, it is about time you got here. We are going to be late to the party," says Myla.

"You know how to make up time, Myla. You have done it many times before."

"Tom, I am not going to speed to get to the party. I just will not 'dilly-dally' at stoplights."

"Now you are talking, Myla."

---

"Bye, honey. You have fun at Cindy's party and remember to stay on the sidewalks," says Ron.

"I will daddy," says Samantha.

"Give me a kiss before you go, sweetheart!"

"Tom, my mother, does not want you riding in the front seat when I am driving," says Myla.

"But, what do you say, Myla?"

"It will be all right with me as long as you keep your hands to yourself."

"I guess you were serious when you said you wouldn't be 'dilly-dallying' Myla."

"Tom, I just anticipate when the red lights turn green with my foot on the gas peddle and the brake pedal. The tires squeal a little, but at least we will get to the party on time."

"Slow down around the corner, Myla."

"Tom, leave me alone. I am completely in control…"

"Now I am in complete control," says Tom as he quickly reaches over and slips his hand under Myla's skirt, resting his hand between her legs.

"Tom, stop it! I told you….."

"Watch out for that tree, Myla!"

"Oh, shit!" exclaims Myla when swerving around the tree and seeing a little girl on the sidewalk in front of her car.

"Quick! Slam on the brake, Myla! Don't hit her!"

"I can't stop, Tom! Oh no…..!"

Myla's car jumps up onto the sidewalk and pins Samantha under her vehicle before coming to a stop.

"Tom, I can't look! Did I hit that little girl?" asks Myla.

"I don't think so. I don't see the little girl anywhere."

"Get out of the car, Tom, and look."

"Myla! The little girl is under the car! There is blood all over!"

"Is she alive, Tom?"

"I don't think so, Myla. I will crawl under the car and see."

"Tom, wait a minute! What is that over there next to the tree I almost hit?"

"Oh, shit! Oh, shit!"

"What is it, Tom?"

"Myla, it is her head. She is decapitated!"

Back at Ronald Tier's home, there is a knock at his door.

"Mr. Ronald Tier?"

"Yes, officer, what can I do for you?"

"Sir, there has been an accident…"

"Oh, no, is it my little Samantha?"

"We are not sure, sir. We will need you to come to the morgue for identification."

Ron travels with the officer to the morgue.

"I want to remind you, Mr. Tier, the girl is quite disfigured," says the officer.

"Officer, I can't make an identification! Where is this girl's head?"

"Over here sir, Is this your daughter?"

"Oh, no! My little Samantha. I told her not to walk on the street! I told her…she is all I have! My poor little girl," cries Ron.

"Mr. Tier, your little girl was not walking on the road. It appears she was walking on the sidewalk when a car lost control and ran up onto the sidewalk," says the officer.

"How the hell did that happen? Who did it?" asks Ron.

"We have a young woman and are questioning her now. So far, her alibi is that she slid to avoid hitting a tree and didn't see your daughter coming around the tree on the sidewalk."

"I want her booked for murder! That's what it is murder!" exclaims Ron.

"Hold on, Mr. Tier, we haven't come to that conclusion yet. It appears that the young woman swerved due to some mechanical issue with her car."

"I don't believe it! That bitch probably was speeding and couldn't make a corner, or something!" exclaims Ron.

"Mr. Tier, you cannot make conclusions like that. We have not finished speaking to her or checked out her car. I suggest you calm down and go home. You will need to make arrangements for your daughter."

"I want to see that woman!" exclaims Ron.

"I am sorry, sir. That will not be possible."

---

Ron purposely buys the following day's newspaper to see if more information has been uncovered about his daughters' death.

"Well, well, well, the woman's name is here in the paper," mutters Ron as he opens the newspaper and reads an article covering the incident.

"It shouldn't be too difficult to get her address.....," Ron speaks to himself.

# MYLA SNEER

There is a heated discussion at the Sneer residence.

"Myla, what the hell happened? You killed a little girl!" exclaims Wanda Sneer.

"I know. I know! Don't you think I feel like a murderer?"

"Are you a murderer, Myla?"

"Mom, I did not see that little girl! The car was heading for a tree, and I swerved. I didn't see her!"

"Why were you going to hit a tree? Were you driving too fast? Was it your friend Tom?"

"Mother, I would rather not say."

"You better say, because you already have 'one foot' in jail, and the police are not done with you yet!"

"Mom, I told Tom to keep his hands to himself while I was driving and all of a sudden he reached over and lifted my skirt while putting his hand between my legs."

"What the hell you telling me, Myla? How could he do that from the back seat, and why would he be so brazen to do a thing like that unless it was a common thing you two do together."

"He was riding in the front seat. I told him he could if he would keep his hands to himself."

"What did I tell you about him riding in the car with you while you were driving? That's right, and he is to only be in the back seat. So, he was trying to grab your crotch, and what did you do?"

"I jumped. It startled me, and I told Tom to stop. I must have jerked the steering wheel because I found myself heading for the tree."

"Did you tell this story to the police, young lady?"

"No, not the exact story."

"You are going to have to tell them what happened. It is too bad for you, but you will have to face the consequences. You were negligent and killed a little girl!"

"I thought you would be a little more sympathetic, mother! Tom is the one at fault!"

"No, Myla. You were driving the car!"

"You just don't care about me!" exclaims Myla angrily.

"Where are you going, Myla?"

"I am going for a walk, and you can't stop me! And, oh, by the way, I have spread my legs many times for Tom. There, are you satisfied?"

Myla opens the house door and slams it behind her.

# RONALD TIER'S REVENGE

Ronald Tier has read every article the newspaper had on the incident that killed his daughter. He is very clever and with a little searching on the Internet, finds that Myla Sneer is the driver of the car; her address and what she looks like.

---

Ron is just turning the corner from Bickson Street to Ripper Street, where Myla lives. He slowly drives down the street and notices a young lady further down, walking on the sidewalk towards him. Ron stops his car, gets out, and starts slowly walking towards the young lady. It isn't long before he recognizes this girl to be Myla Sneer. Ron slows his pace but continues to walk towards her. As he is walking, he thinks she is about twenty years old; a little over four feet in height and weighing about one hundred twenty pounds. Ron thinks to himself, "No problem. I have carried men twice her weight in 'Nam.'"

Just as Ron passes by Myla, he grabs her around the waist with one arm and places his other hand across her mouth to muffle her screams.

"Listen bitch. I won't hurt you unless you struggle. You are coming with me," says Ron.

---

Ron lifts Myla and places her across his shoulders in a fashion to keep her mouth closed against his shoulder. She tries to bite him, but he twists her arm behind her until she stops. He carries her to his car and puts her in the front seat, placing a gag in her mouth. He then ties her hands together and fastens the seatbelt around her.

Ron takes Myla to his house and carries her to the basement. In the far corner, a mattress lies on the floor, and chains hanging from the upper floor rafters. A type of sling lies directly above the mattress bed.

---

"This is your new home, and if you scream, I will put the gag back in your mouth. I want to tell you why you are here," says Ron.

"Let me go, you bastard! What do you want from me?" asks Myla.

"I read in the newspaper the other day that someone hit and killed a little girl with their car," says Ron.

"So, what does that have to do with me," says Myla.

"That little girl was my daughter!" exclaims Ron.

"I am sorry. I hope the police got the person who killed your daughter," says Myla.

"They didn't, but I did!"

"No, you have the wrong person!" exclaims Myla.

"No, I don't, and you know it!"

"So, what are you going to do with me?" questions Myla.

"I have you shackled in these chains so you cannot escape. The basement is your bedroom from now on. I will bring you your meals," says Ron.

"Oh, so you are placing me in your 'jail'?"

"You are going to replace my daughter who you murdered!"

"Well, seeing your daughter was about twelve years old, and I am twenty. I don't think I will replace her."

"Think again, sweetheart. You aren't the replacement, but you are going to give me her replacement," says Ron.

"Just wait a minute, buster. Are you talking about me birthing your replacement daughter?"

"Bullseye! You hit the jackpot!"

"Hell no! There is no way in hell I am going to let you fuck me to get me pregnant with your child 'replacement'."

"It doesn't appear you have a choice, now does it?"

"I would rather die first!"

"On the contrary, you will live and give me my daughter back. It won't be like you are thinking. I won't be having sex with you, per se. I won't even penetrate you with my penis."

"Oh, so you discovered the secret to immaculate conception?" asks Myla.

"No, take a look in this refrigerator. What do we have here? It looks like semen to me, my semen. You see that apparatus hanging above you, well, that will hoist you up at the correct angle for probable conception after I insert my semen into your vagina with this turkey baster."

"You are a sick bastard! I won't let you insert that into my pussy!"

"You don't have a choice. You are shackled in a way you can't resist me hooking you up to the sling. I won't even have to pull your panties down. I will just cut a slit into them. After all, I am not interested in seeing your pussy! I need it as a vehicle to get my daughter back."

"You will never get away with this! I won't carry your baby! I won't! I will kill it somehow!"

"You won't succeed. Let's give it a shot right now," says Ron.

"I am going to scream!" exclaims Myla.

"OK, I will put the gag back in your mouth," says Ronald.

Ron skillfully lowers the sling apparatus as he hoists one leg and one arm on her same side to flip Myla on her stomach. He then slides the sling under her and raises the two chains, one on each of her legs, higher to have Myla's head lower than her ass. Those same two chains are moved away from each other, resulting in spreading her legs.

Ron picks up the scalpel and carefully cuts a slit in Myla's panties to allow access to her vagina. Ron then goes to the bench where he had previously taken the jar of his semen out of the refrigerator to warm. He lowers the turkey baster into it and draws about a teaspoon amount into it.

Myla is moaning and crying through the gag in her mouth, but Ron ignores her as he spreads the labia of her vagina and inserts the baster while slowly squeezing out its contents.

Myla lets out one last gasp as she feels the warm semen settle into her vagina.

# THE HARFORD POLICE DEPARTMENT GETS INVOLVED

C hief Julia Lillus is returning from a long weekend and is checking with her receptionist, Betsy, on recent events in Harford.

"Betsy, is there anything needing immediate attention this morning?" asks Julia.

"No, but I have heard there is a missing girl alert over in Lewis County. They say a twenty-year-old went for a walk and hasn't been seen for a couple of days," says Betsy.

"That is too bad. I hope they find her. There are a lot of crazy people out there. Betsy, I am going to forward my direct calls to you for the morning. I have a lot of paperwork to file."

"OK, Julia."

Julia relishes the time in the morning before Bobbie and Richard show up. The uninterrupted quietness allows her to catch up on her ever-increasing case filing. She hopes for a quiet day in Harford.

---

"Julia, I hate to bother you, but a Chief of Police from the Lewis County Police Department is on the line wishing to speak to you," says Betsy.

"Thank you, Betsy, pass his call over."

"Hello, this is Julia Lillus. I am the Chief of Police for the Harford Police Department. What can I do for you?"

"Hi, my name is Chief Ronald Marble from the Lewis County Police Department. You have probably heard we have a missing woman over here in the town of Kingsley?"

"Yes, I heard about it. How is that missing persons going? Have you found her yet?"

"No, it is why I am calling you. You and your Police Department have quite a reputation for cracking cases. We feel there may be more than just a 'runaway' with this missing woman."

"I appreciate the compliment. How would you like us to proceed?"

"Chief Lillus."

"Please call me Julia. I am not a very formal person."

"Sure, Julia. Because of your excellent reputation and the addition of your Forensics Lab, I would be grateful if you and your Department handled the case entirely. We can be of assistance if need be."

"Well, Chief, I am honored to have you ask this of us, but it is out of our jurisdiction and the County…"

"Julia, I have that all taken care of with your City and County officials. I believe they recommended you and your Department as well."

"OK, what details do you have?"

"Julia, this case is a little sticky. The woman missing had hit and killed a little girl with her car last Monday. We have been working on the details, but it appears as negligence was the reason. It didn't go well with her family, and an argument went on between her and her mother. The twenty-year-old stormed out of her house and said she was going for a walk. She has not been seen or heard from since then."

"Is there anyone she may have had contact with that might know of her whereabouts?" asks Julia.

"She was with a boyfriend at the time of the car incident. He hasn't seen or heard from her since our questioning."

"OK, Chief, email to me contacts and the address of her mother. We will get on it immediately, and I will keep you informed of our progress," says Julia.

---

Richard, Bobbie, and Amanda arrive at the office. They notice Julia hanging up her phone with a pad of paper with notes written.

---

"Good morning Julia," says Bobbie.

"Good morning to all of you; as soon as you get settled in, I would like you to meet me in the conference room. We have an interesting case before us."

---

"We have been asked to handle a missing person case for Lewis County."

"Lewis County," says Richard.

"Yes, because our Department is so efficient and we now have a Forensics Lab, thanks to Amanda, we are becoming the 'go-to' Police Department of choice. What we have here is a twenty-year-old woman who has been involved in an automobile incident leaving a little girl dead. The Police Department in Kingsley has determined negligence on her part. She and her mother argued, and she left home for a walk. No one has seen or heard from her in several days. Besides her mother wanting her to return home, I suspect the Police Depart-

41

ment wants her for further questioning and a possible booking," says Julia.

"It is possible she is running because she knows her negligence led to the cause of death, and she could end up with a conviction," says Bobbie.

"Very true, Bobbie," says Julia.

"All three of us will travel to Kingsley, and Amanda, I will possibly need your expertise. I have a feeling something is going on much deeper than it appears."

"Oh, here we go again. Julia has a hunch," says Richard.

"Yes, and Julia is usually correct with her hunches," says Bobbie.

"I will go talk to her mother. Richard, I want you to scout around town and see what information you can find on possible 'whereabouts' this woman may be or where she might have been. Bobbie, I want you to research the family of the little girl who was killed and get their general attitude. See if anyone in the family has a revengeful emotion. I have some paperwork to complete. Richard and Bobbie, you can get started over to Kingsley. I will be there in a couple of hours," says Julia.

# ARE YOU PREGNANT?

R onald Tier is returning from the drugstore and walks down to the basement.

---

"Here you go, honey. Take this and do what you need to do," says Ron.

"What! A pregnancy test? Hell, no, I won't take it," says Myla.

"You will! I will continue placing my semen in your pussy until you do!" exclaims Ron.

"You will have to let me go to the bathroom for this."

"Fine, but there must not be any funny business! I want to see the results of the test."

"Why don't you just come in and watch me pee, you bastard!"

"Just get in there and do what you need to do. Remember, I am right outside this door with a gun. Pass the test out to me when you are finished. I will shackle you and see if we need to use the turkey baster again."

Myla reluctantly passes the pregnancy test over to Ron's outstretched hand.

———

"Well, I see you are not pregnant yet. Let's try again."

———

Myla is once again gagged, hoisted in the sling with her ass higher than her head, on her stomach.

She feels the warmth of Ron's semen, as Ron slides the turkey baster in her vagina and squeezes the rubber bulb.

# JULIA AND MRS. SNEER HAVE A TALK

J ulia arrives at Myla's home to interview her mother, Wanda
Sneer.

---

"Hello, Mrs. Sneer? I am Chief Julia Lillus from the Harford Police
Department. Would you mind answering a few questions? I am
working to find your daughter and bring her back to you safely."

"Yes, please do come in. My name is Wanda Sneer, and my daughter's name is Myla."

"Tell me what happened, Mrs. Sneer."

"As you probably know, Myla crashed her car and hit a little girl.
The little girl died. Myla and her boyfriend Tom were going to a
party. Myla was driving, and Tom was supposed to be in the back seat
when Myla is driving. Tom can't keep his hands to himself. For some
reason, Myla allowed Tom to sit in the passenger seat even though I
gave her strict orders about that. I was able to get from Myla that Tom
suddenly reached over and slipped his hand under her skirt and
started to caress her and well, you know. She jerked the steering
wheel in surprise and headed for a tree. To miss hitting the tree, she

swerved, and I guess the little girl was out of sight on the sidewalk behind the tree until she swerved and ran over the little girl."

"She told you all of this?" asks Julia.

"Yes, and when I started to scold her and I had asked her if she thought about the seriousness of what she was involved in, she got immediately defensive and angry. I reminded her of my mistrust of Tom. The last thing she said to me before storming out the door was that she had spread her legs many times for Tom."

"Why did she say that to you? What did that have to do with the automobile incident?"

"Well, you see Chief, Myla had always told me Tom was just a friend, and there was nothing between them. I pressed her to tell me why 'just a friend' would reach for her crotch to caress it. That is when she said what I just told you and when I found out they were having sexual relations. That girl! I brought her up better than that!"

"Did your daughter, Myla, tell you where she was going?"

"No, she just angrily said she was going for a walk and slammed the door behind her."

"Thank you for your time, Mrs. Sneer. I will be in touch with you if I need more information or find where your daughter has gone."

---

Julia leaves the home of Mrs. Sneer and pulls out her notes to find Tom's home address.

# TOM AND HIS FATHER

J ulia arrives at Tom's house.

---

"Hello, sir. I am Chief Julia Lillus from the Harford Police Department. Is your son, Tom, home? I would like to speak with him, if I may," says Julia.

"Why the hell you police harassing my son? He didn't kill that girl. It was that Sneer bitch!"

"I only want to question your son if he has any idea where the Sneer girl is."

"He doesn't!"

"Sir, I need to question your son Tom. Please call him to the door."

"Hey, Tom! I have another police that wants to question you. She ain't bad looking for a cop!"

"Hello, Tom. My name is Chief Julia Lillus, and I would like to ask if you know where the Sneer girl went or if you have heard from her?"

"No, I don't. I heard she ran away from home shortly after the accident."

"Do you have any idea where she might have gone?"

"No, I do not. It is unusual that Myla hasn't contacted me. We are quite close."

"Yes, I heard that from her mother."

"Her mother doesn't know the half of it!"

"I think she does; her daughter told her about the sexual relations you two are sharing and that you startled her daughter trying to fondle her…," says Julia.

"My boy wouldn't do such a thing unless she wanted it," says Tom's father.

"Do you think she wanted it while she was driving, sir?" asks Julia.

"Look, miss 'good looking' I taught my boy well. He found a girl he likes; he fondles her up to see if she is receptive and screws her without getting her 'knocked up.'"

"I am not here to discuss the teaching lessons you have or haven't given your son or Tom's relationship with this girl. I am asking for any information that may lead to where she is. The local Police Department will handle the rest," says Julia.

Julia turns from the door to leave when Tom's father hollers to her.

"Tell the local police I thank them for sending a lady cop to my house with such an inviting ass."

Julia mumbles to herself, "Don't turn around; don't answer back; just keep walking with my tight ass."

---

Julia completes what she planned and drives back to her office, hoping Richard and Bobbie have information on the case.

# BACK AT THE POLICE DEPARTMENT

J ulia catches up with Richard and Bobbie to find out what information they have on the case.

---

"Bobbie, what did you find out?" asks Julia.

"I found out the little girl who was killed is Samantha Tier, and she was about twelve years old. Her mother died years ago with cancer when the little girl was just a baby. She lived with her father, a Vietnam Vet, and he thought the world of her. His name is Ronald Tier. I guess he was quite grief-stricken when his wife passed," says Bobbie.

"I am sure he is devastated over the loss of his daughter," says Julia.

"I found out this Ronald Tier became a recluse after his wife passed. He only is seen when out buying groceries or clothes for his now-deceased daughter," says Richard.

"How about around town? Did you find anything else?"

"No, Julia, just what I told you," says Richard.

# RONALD LOSES ANOTHER CHILD

It is time for another pregnancy test for Ron's captive, Myla.

---

"Hand me that test when you have finished," says Ron.

"Listen, you bastard, why don't you just come in here and retrieve it yourself? What is the difference; you have already seen my pussy and raped me with the turkey baster," says Myla.

"I told you, I am not interested in seeing your pussy or having sex with you. I just want you to give me my daughter back," says Ron.

"Here, pig! Sorry, I peed on it!" exclaims Myla.

"You are in luck, dear. I won't need to pull out the turkey baster. It appears you are pregnant."

"What if it isn't a girl?"

"It will be a girl," says Ron.

"So you are going to keep me shackled for nine months? You must have a lot of patience," says Myla.

"If you behave, I will undo your shackles and treat you like any mother-to-be, but you will have to live down here in the basement. I will fix this area up just for you, like an apartment. Now, I have to go out and get some nutritional items for the mother of my baby girl," says Ron.

---

As soon as Ron leaves his home and Myla, she starts to devise a plan to escape. As she recalls past days, Ron seems to enter and leave the house from the basement through the Bilco® style doors and never the basement door to the first floor of the home. Myla calculates how far it is from the mattress bed to the basement stairs to the first floor of the house and how fast she needs to run to get there, ahead of Ron. She is going to wait until he returns from the grocery store and has to go up to the kitchen to unpack the groceries. Myla is counting on Ron releasing her shackles and forgetting to lock the basement door when he returns to her bedside.

Myla suddenly hears Ron unlocking the door and entering the basement with an armful of bagged groceries.

---

"Sweetheart, I bought a whole bunch of fruits and vegetables for you to eat. My daughter needs to be healthy from the start," says Ron.

"Ron, I have been thinking, and I realize the hurt I have caused you. I feel having your baby is the only way I can make it up to you. I want to be a friend to you and do whatever you wish to give you your daughter back," says Myla.

"Well, we are getting somewhere. I promise I will take care of you and give you all you need to care for my daughter."

"Do you think the shackles can be removed from my ankles? They hurt, and because of my pregnancy, they are a little swollen, and I have to tone myself. To do that, I will need my legs free. Besides, you can keep me handcuffed, and you lock all of the doors. I promise I won't cause you any trouble. I want to deliver your daughter to you."

"Sounds good to me. There, your shackles are removed, and you can do what you need to strengthen yourself. I will be right back. I need to put these groceries away, and I will be back down to discuss what type of meals you would like."

"There is one more thing," says Myla.

"What is it?"

"I will be with you for nine months. Don't you think they will be looking for me? Also, I will not enter into sexual relations with you. I won't give you oral sex, vaginal intercourse, or anything involving your sexual desires. You 'knocked me up,' and there will be nothing more."

"No one will ever be able to trace you here, and after nine months, you can return to your life. Don't worry! If I had wanted sexual relations with you, I sure as hell wouldn't have used a turkey baster, I would have fucked you with my cock. I told you my wish was not to have you as my whore; I just want you to give me my daughter back."

---

Ron leaves Myla to go up to the kitchen. She hears him unlock the door but does not hear him re-lock it. Myla immediately runs over to under the stairs and waits for his return so she can rush up the stairs to freedom. She plans to get his attention by creating an emergency.

---

"Help! Help! I am having deep pain in my stomach! Oh, the baby!" yells Myla.

Ron flings open the basement door and rushes down the stairs. As soon as he clears the stairway and begins to rush over to Myla's mattress bed, Myla runs from under the stairwell and runs to the top of the stairs. Ron immediately notices Myla's fleeing and starts to run following her up the stairway.

"You bitch! I knew I should have never trusted you. Get back down here!" exclaims Ron as he catches up to Myla and grabs her hand.

"No, No, you bastard! Let me go!"

"No chance," Ron says as he pulls at Myla.

Just as Myla is forced to turn around to descend the stairs, her ankle twists, and she trips on one of the steps, losing her balance and falls toward Ron.

"Oh, shit!" says Ron as Myla falls into him, and he loses his balance.

---

They both tumble down the stairway, and as Myla rolls off of Ron when they both hit the basement floor, she hits the baluster with her head; a loud crack is heard, and blood immediately starts to flow from her skull. Myla lay lifeless at the bottom of the stairs while Ron rights himself from the fall.

---

"Get up, bitch! You aren't going anywhere, and the shackles are returning to your ankles. Now get up!"

---

Myla does not move, and Ron checks to see how bad she is hurt. As he starts to lift her, her head immediately falls to her shoulder at an angle that is not natural.

---

"Oh, shit! Her neck is broke! My daughter...my daughter," Ron mutters as he weeps.

---

Ron experiences rage as well as heartbrokenness. His mind is so cluttered he starts to give Myla CPR followed by mouth-to-mouth respiration in hopes of reviving her. He wonders if he can get her to the hospital quick enough to save his baby. Myla is over a month pregnant and is just starting to show a noticeable baby bump. If he goes to the hospital with Myla, there will be all sorts of questions that he cannot answer without revealing what he has done to her.

———

"I cannot risk it. Sweetheart, please wake up," says Ron.

———

Myla's head bobs uncontrollably with her broken neck, but Ron is not thinking clearly enough to realize that whatever he does to revive her, she will not wake up. She is dead, and so is her baby.

An hour passes, and Ron starts to get a clear head and realizes that Myla is gone, and so is his baby.

———

"Now I have to start all over again. I will need to find me another mother for my daughter, but first I have to get rid of this body," Ron mutters to himself.

# DISPOSE OF THE BODY

Ron places Myla in the trunk of his car after wrapping her in a plastic garbage bag and attaching a cinder block so she will sink in the pond. When darkness falls, Ron starts his car and drives off to Crippen Pond, where he will dispose of the body.

---

"No one will ever find her before the crayfish finish their feasting," says Ron.

---

After Ron disposes of Myla in the pond, he drives back to his home. When he arrives, he cleans up the blood on his basement floor and makes ready the mattress for the new mother of his child. Ron then goes into the particular room where he unzips his pants and stares at the nude women pictures on the wall, bent over, exposing their wide-open pussies. After a few strokes on his penis, he ejaculates into a mason jar. He places the jar in the refrigerator.

"I have to do this for the next mother of my daughter, but it sure does feel good. Maybe I should stop using the turkey baster and fuck her with my cock. No, that wouldn't be right. I don't want to rape her. Besides, I got enough pussy from that sixteen-year-old 'Cong' girl. What a pussy she had; I should have found a way to get her over here after the war," says Ron as he starts to dream about his experiences in the past.

# AMANDA

Julia calls Bobbie, Richard, and Amanda into her office for a briefing.

---

"OK guys, Mrs. Sneer's daughter, Myla, has not shown up at her home. Has anyone of you found further clues to her disappearance?" asks Julia.

"No, but I was talking to a clerk at the local grocery down the road from Sneer's home, and she said there was a guy who usually comes into the store once a month to purchase his groceries and noticed that he has started to come into the store weekly. She also said that the items he has purchased were much more nutritious than his usual purchases," says Bobbie.

"Maybe he is starting a new health regimen," says Amanda.

"Amanda, would you please take a trip to Mrs. Sneer's home and visit her? I have a hunch we will need some DNA samples of her daughters'. Do your magic and don't alarm Mrs. Sneer," says Julia.

"No problem! A bathroom break is all I need while visiting," says Amanda.

"Pardon my lack of knowledge, Amanda, but how long can we keep the DNA sample before it is no longer good?" asks Julia.

"That will not be a problem because once I get the sample, I will immediately run the tests and then the results will be logged digitally in the lab database for future use," says Amanda.

———

Amanda gets her required paperwork and starts to travel to Mrs. Sneer's home.

———

"Hello Mrs. Sneer, my name is Amanda Alexandria from the Harford Police Department. I thought while I was in the area, I would stop and visit you to see if you have heard from your daughter, Myla."

"Oh, hello, I have not heard from her or anything about where she could be. Everything is quiet around here except down the road a bit at Crippen Pond," says Mrs. Sneer.

"Why, what is going on down there?" asks Amanda.

"I don't know, but there are a lot of people down there, and I have seen at least two squad cars race past my house. Probably someone fell into the pond again."

"Does that often happen, Mrs. Sneer?"

"Yes, the kids around here like to go crayfish hunting and usually end up in the pond one way or another. The bottom is all mud, and they sometimes get their feet stuck and can't move. Kind of like quicksand except they don't keep sinking. My Myla, when she was just a kid, used to go fishing down there and get stuck in the mud. My husband used to have to go and pull her out. I wish Myla was in the pond at this moment. I would relish her missing only to be found stuck in the pond."

"Mrs. Sneer, would you excuse me. I will need to visit your bathroom before I head back to my office," says Amanda.

"Sure, it is down the hall on the right. Can I fix you some tea?"

"Sure, that would be splendid. I don't need to go back to the office right away."

---

Amanda enters the bathroom and closes the door. While she relieves herself, she looks around at the sink counter and immediately notices a pink toothbrush. The stars must be in the correct alignment because on the handle of the toothbrush is the name 'Myla'. She scraps the bristles and bags the sample.

---

"Amanda, here is your tea. Would you like some sugar?"

"No, that is fine. It is good the way it is."

"Amanda, would you mind if I talked to you a bit about Myla?"

"No not at all. Sometimes it helps in situations such as this to talk about it."

"I don't want you or your Department to think my Myla is a whore. We brought her up better than that."

"Mrs. Sneer, a sexual encounter with a boy, doesn't label one as a whore. I am sure Myla is very selective with whom she sleeps with, and I am sure she isn't sleeping with every guy that passes her way."

"Yes, but the boy…that boy is not good for her. He has no manners. This whole mess started because he couldn't keep his hands off her crotch."

"Mrs. Sneer, it will not do you any good to dwell on the past. It is unfortunate, but we must look ahead and work on finding your daughter. That is where our energy needs to be spent."

"I suppose you are right, Amanda."

"Mrs. Sneer, time sure has flown by, and I must get back to the office. Thank you for the tea. If you hear any information about your daughter's whereabouts, please get in touch with Chief Julia, and we will also pass on to you any new information we find."

"Thanks so much for stopping by Amanda. It is quite lonely with me just being here and nothing I can do about the situation. Could I ask you a question?"

"Sure."

"Have you married Amanda?"

"No, I haven't. I guess I am just too busy with my job."

"Such a shame to waste that beauty you have and not share it with the right guy."

"Thank you. Someday, maybe," says Amanda.

---

Amanda decides to take a trip down the road to find Crippen Pond and see what is going on. As she approaches the pond, she sees a couple of squad cars and quite a few bystanders. She stops and gets out of the vehicle.

---

"Hi, my name is Amanda Alexandria from the Harford Police Department."

"Thank God you are here. We were just about to call your office," says one of the local police officers.

"What is going on?" asks Amanda.

"We have pulled a body from the pond. It is an apparent homicide. The girl is wrapped in a plastic bag with a severed cord, which appears to have been attached to a cinder block. Those crayfish did a good job on her. We can see she is a young girl and by the looks of it, pregnant unless she is just bloated from being under the water," says the officer.

"Is the coroner on the way?" asks Amanda.

"Yes, he has been called."

"Do you mind if I go over and take a look at the body?" asks Amanda.

"Sure, go ahead. The girl is not a great sight to see. The crayfish...."

Amanda walks over to the body and flashes her Department Badge to the other officer. She bends down to survey the body and is glad to see the girl's mouth is closed. She places her fingers on the girl's lips and spreads them to open her mouth. Amanda takes a swab from her Forensics Case and swabs the inside cheeks of the girl.

"I will call this into our office. We are handling the missing Sneer girl's case, and this discovery may help us in the investigation; it might even be her," says Amanda to the officer.

"Julia, this is Amanda. There is a body that has shown up here, near Mrs. Sneer's home. I feel it is valuable for our case on her missing daughter. I have gotten DNA samples from the body, and I will be returning to the office momentarily."

"Thanks, Amanda. I will send Richard over there to handle the situation. Richard, go down to Mrs. Sneer's house and see what you can find out about the body they found in a Crippen Pond. It is just down the road from her house," says Julia.

"I am on it, Julia."

"Take Bobbie with you if she isn't busy. And, Richard, leave Bobbie alone. Remember she is a pregnant mommy," says Julia.

"Keeping that 'oven' full."

"Richard!" exclaims Julia.

At the Harford Police Department, Amanda has returned and running the DNA samples from the body found at Crippen Pond. On a hunch, she compares the results from the results taken from Myla's toothbrush.

---

"Julia, could you please come to my office," says Amanda.

"Yes surely."

"Julia, we have found the missing girl. The DNA analysis from Mrs. Sneer's daughter's toothbrush match that of the body found in Crippen Pond."

"I had a hunch that would be the case. It was just a feeling. I also just received a call from the local Police Department down there, and they gave me the name and phone number to the coroner who handles their cases. The report from the coroner's first glance is a girl in her early twenties, and she was pregnant; over a month," says Julia.

"Oh, no! I wonder if the father is that boyfriend, Tom," says Amanda.

"Amanda, I already arranged with the coroner for you to go and get samples of her vaginal tissues for DNA testing. Once we tell this tragedy to Mrs. Sneer and the boyfriend's father, we will need to pull the boyfriend in and get DNA samples from him. I will get the boyfriend here for questioning and sampling. I do not want to expose you to his father. That man practically raped me with his eyes while I was questioning him earlier," says Julia.

"I guess that is what we get for being a 'sexy woman' Police Department, except for Richard," says Amanda laughingly.

"Don't worry about Richard. He is too busy keeping Bobbie busy with babies. He recognizes only one sexy woman from this Police Department. Poor Bobbie!" exclaims Julia.

"It appears Bobbie doesn't mind being 'barefoot and pregnant'," says Amanda.

"No, she doesn't. She is just as much at fault as Richard is. Neither one can keep their hands off each other. They certainly are a 'horny pair'."

"I love watching them interact. Someday I might be able to be in the same spot," says Amanda.

"In time, Amanda, I am sure it will happen. Now, I got to get over to Mrs. Sneer and break the news to her. I will get the boyfriend here, also."

# ARE YOU THE FATHER OF THE BABY?

Julia travels to Mrs. Sneer's home to tell her the bad news about her daughter being found dead in Crippen Pond. She leaves Mrs. Sneer trembling and in tears but left out of the conversation that her daughter was pregnant.

---

Julia pulls up to Tom's home and readies herself to meet his 'rapist' father. She tried not to wear any provocative outfits for this visit but realizes it doesn't matter because he 'undresses' her with his eyes.

---

"What the hell you doing back here?"

"I am Chief Julia…"

"I know who you are. You are that sexy cop from Harford."

"Look, please keep your sexual harassment comments to yourself. I would like to speak to your son Tom," says Julia.

"Well, well, a broad who doesn't like comments. Tom, the sexy Police Officer, is here to see you," says Tom's father.

"Tom, I need you to come with me to my office for questioning," says Julia.

"What the hell for? He isn't involved with that slut Sneer girl," says Tom's father.

"In case you haven't heard, they found the Sneer girl in the Crippen Pond yesterday," says Julia.

"Is she dead? Serves her right," says Tom's father.

"Tom, please come with me. I will be bringing you back home when I am finished."

"No way! He is not going with you, missy. My boy is not going to be questioned without me being there with him," says Tom's father.

"Suit yourself, but I will not put up with your sexual remarks towards me. If I hear any, I will bring a sexual harassment case against you, and it won't be pretty," says Julia.

"OK, OK, but you should relish in how you look to us, males!"

"Get in the car and say nothing," says Julia.

---

Back at the Harford Police Department, Julia leads Tom and his father into her office. Tom's father happens to notice Amanda at the copier and begins to 'rape' her with his eyes.

---

"Hell, I need a job here! All you ladies are 'good lookers'....seriously hot."

"I am warning you," says Julia.

"I am just giving your Department personnel a compliment."

---

"Tom, I have told you Myla Sneer was found dead in the Crippen Pond. She was weighted down by a cinder block. She appears to have been dead before she was put into the pond. Tom, I must ask you what your relationship was to the Sneer girl?" asks Julia.

"Well, she wasn't my girlfriend. I did enjoy being with her," says Tom.

"Tom were you and the Sneer girl sharing sexual relations?" asks Julia.

"Objection! My son doesn't have to answer that question!" exclaims Tom's father.

"Sir, this is not a court, and Tom must answer the question. The Sneer girl was pregnant."

"Oh no! My son is not the father," says Tom's father.

"I could be the father. We had been sexually experimenting a few times," says Tom.

"Tom, the only way we can know this is with a DNA test. Are you willing to have the test?"

"Yes, I guess so. I will have to jerk off in front of you?" asks Tom.

"If you have to jerk off in front of anyone, Tom, pick that babe in that office over there," says Tom's father.

"Well, sir, you are now duly charged with sexual harassment. I warned you!" exclaims Julia.

"Tom, that will not be necessary. All we need is to scrap on the inside of your cheek with a cotton swab."

"OK, I can do that," says Tom.

"Great! Please go over to that office, and Amanda, our Forensics Specialist, will help you with the sampling," says Julia.

"Now, Mr.?" asks Julia.

"My name is Tom Windsley, ma'am."

"Mr. Windsley, in that you cannot keep your comments to yourself, I have two choices for you. You can spend a few days in jail and pay a fine of two hundred dollars for sexual harassment involving my Department personnel, or I can let you go with a fine of five hundred dollars. Which would you prefer?"

"That is a pretty steep fine."

"You can't say I did not warn you. I gave you many chances to clean your mouth, but you refused," says Julia.

"I am so sorry, ma'am. You see, I haven't been with a woman in such a long time since my wife passed on, and I guess all of it just filled me up until it spilled over."

"Sir, I know that you intended to flatter my Officer and me, but you are lucky you made those remarks to me. I am letting you off easy. If you were to say those types of remarks to Amanda over there or another female and she were to bring charges to you, you would be in court and possibly in jail. Also, you might want to realize that the remarks you have made shows to me you just might act out on those feelings and physically harm someone, or even rape."

"No, no, I would never do that."

"Let this be a lesson, Mr. Windsley. What route do you want to take?"

"I will pay you the five hundred dollars for my stupidity. I can't miss a day from work."

"Mr. Windsley, I don't want your money. I want you to give that money to Mrs. Sneer for your son's part in her daughters' death; the car accident partially caused by your son surprising the Sneer girl by grabbing her inappropriately."

"Yes, ma'am, I will do that."

"It will be on your conscience. I will be checking to see if you turn the money over to Mrs. Sneer," says Julia.

"Ma'am, may I say something as a gentleman?"

"Surely."

"Even though my remarks were inappropriate, deep down, I wanted to compliment you on your beauty and how I am pleased you are running a Police Department."

"Thank you, Mr. Windsley. Did we learn something today?"

"Yes, ma'am, I did."

"Good, Tom is done, and if you don't mind, take a seat out in the reception area, and we will have the DNA results shortly," says Julia.

"Ma'am, what if the results show Tom is the father?"

"We will cross that bridge if we need to. Amanda, do you have the results from Tom's DNA test?" asks Julia.

"I am almost finished. Just a couple of minutes more."

Amanda steps from her office with the test results in her hand as she approaches Tom and his father.

"Tom, you have already met Amanda. Mr. Windsley, this is Amanda. She is our Forensics Specialist, and she is going to go over the test results with you and Tom," says Julia.

"Hello, ma'am, it is nice to meet you," says Mr. Windsley.

"Tom, your DNA test results came back negative to you being the father of the Sneer girls' baby. We could do a more extensive test involving matching your sperm with her vaginal fluids, but I do not feel that necessary. My testing gives strong evidence that you are not the father."

"Thank you, Amanda," says Tom.

"Thank you, Tom, for being so willing to come in for the test," says Amanda.

"Tom were you at any time mad at the Sneer girl for any reason?" asks Julia.

"No ma'am, I liked her a lot. I wouldn't do anything to bring her pain."

"Did you ever suspect that she might be pregnant and that you were the father?"

"No, ma'am, after we...ugh had sexual relations a few weeks earlier, I asked her if she had had her period. She responded to me that she did and to not worry, and that was the last time we were together before she became missing."

"OK, Mr. Windsley and Tom, I will take you back to your home," says Julia.

# FORENSICS, DNA, ETC.

W hen Julia returns to the Police Department after taking Tom and his father back to their home.

---

"Richard, what did you get from the Crippen Pond scene?" asks Julia.

"Other than the information you already knew from the coroner's report, I did see tire tracks, which may be the vehicle the person used to dump the body. Bobbie and I got a plaster mold of the tread," says Richard.

"Julia, the body, was not undressed, as you know, but the strange thing is that her panties were slit in the area of her vagina. The coroner report states that he felt there was penetration, but I find it hard to believe someone would go to the work of slitting her panties to have sexual relations with her. Why wouldn't they just take her panties off?" asks Bobbie.

"Yeah, that is the way to do it!"

"Richard, keep quiet!" exclaims Bobbie.

"Yes, and Mrs. Sneer said that the clothes her daughter was wearing are the clothes she had on when she stomped out of the house. It appears that she never changed her clothes for over a month in that she was also over a month pregnant. Whoever kidnapped her and made her pregnant didn't bother giving her new clothes; it did appear the clothes had been washed," says Julia.

"So, you are implying she was kidnapped and impregnated by the person who kidnapped her?" asks Bobbie.

"Just a hunch," says Julia.

"Your hunches always seem to turn out to be fact," says Richard.

"Richard, I need you to go to the vicinity of Crippen Pond and look for possible tire tread matches with local cars. We will start there. Amanda, I would like you to go to the coroner's and get a second sample of the Sneer girls vaginal fluid. We might need that to further match other DNA samples. Meanwhile, Bobbie and I have to go meet the birthing class coaches so we can do the required exercises for her birthing. Seeing I am Bobbie's birthing coach, I need to assist her in the exercises," says Julia.

# AMANDA IS STALKED

Amanda travels to the coroner's office but needs to stop at the grocery store to get a protein drink for her lunch before returning to the office.

---

Ron is making his rounds to the grocery store to find his next female to birth his daughter. It just so happens that Amanda and Ron are frequenting the same grocery store. Ron pretends he is looking for healthy snacks. He hangs out in the health food area of the grocery because he knows physically fit good-looking girls frequent that area. After all, Ron wants an attractive girl to birth his daughter because his wife was very attractive and gave him a beautiful daughter. As he turns into the protein shake aisle, he sees Amanda making a selection of protein drinks.

---

"Wow, what a beautiful woman. She has well-sculpted legs and beautiful features in her face. She looks as if she is in her mid-twenties, and she is still young enough to birth children," Ron mutters to himself.

"Oh, I am sorry. Excuse me. I should watch where I am going," says Ron as he slides into Amanda as he passes.

"That is OK. I am kind of sticking out in this aisle looking for protein drinks," says Amanda.

---

Ron notices as he passes Amanda, that she drops a card from her hand. He picks it up and sees it is an address somewhere. He decides to wait for her at the exit door to the grocery store and follow her to her car before revealing the card she dropped.

Amanda checks out from the grocery store, and with a bag in hand, walks to her car. Ron sets a pace behind her, so she doesn't see or suspect him following her. Amanda reaches her car and opens the passenger door to put the bag onto the seat.

---

"Ma'am, I am sorry, but you dropped this when I accidentally bumped into you in the protein aisle," says Ron.

"Oh, yes, thank you. I need that address," says Amanda.

---

Ron makes as if he is leaving as Amanda turns around to close the passenger side door. Ron swiftly comes up behind her and quickly places his hand around from her back to her mouth with a cloth across it. Immediately Amanda slumps into Ron's arms. He lifts her to make it look like she is walking, looking like maybe she is drunk, in order not to draw attention. When Ron gets to his car, he places Amanda in the passenger seat and swiftly drives to his home. At his house, he lifts Amanda over his shoulder and puts his hand on her thigh to hold her skirt down. Down to the basement, Ron places Amanda onto the mattress and attaches the shackles.

---

"Where am I? Who are you, and what is this place? Why am I here?" asks Amanda.

"Quiet now, I will tell you all in due time," says Ron.

"How did you get me down here?"

"Formaldehyde, my dear."

"I am an Officer for the Harford Police Department," says Amanda.

"Great! A smart woman for my daughter," says Ron.

"What do you mean by that?" asks Amanda.

"My daughter was taken from me because of a careless slut who couldn't control her automobile."

"Are you talking about the recent car accident involving a middle school girl?"

"Yes, that was my daughter Samantha."

"What does that have to do with me?"

"Well, my dear, you are going to give my daughter back to me."

"I can't bring your daughter back from the dead. You should know that."

"No, you are going to give birth to my daughter."

"I don't follow. Are you telling me you are going to impregnate me to birth a child for you?"

"Precisely, I had a daughter in the 'oven' with that slut who killed my daughter. She tried to escape and killed herself. Now, I must start all over again with you."

"Mister, whoever you are, you are not going to impregnate me. I will not have sexual intercourse with you!"

"You have no choice, sweetheart! You are shackled so you cannot get away from me and see this harness? Well, that is how it is done. Don't worry. I won't have sexual relations with you. It is not what I want. I just want you to carry my baby. See this turkey baster here? I will impregnate you with my semen entered into your vagina via this baster."

"You will never get away with this. My office will be looking for me."

"By the time they find you, a baby will be in your 'oven'. Then what are they going to do, kill my baby?"

"Supposing your plan works, they will never let you keep your baby daughter because you will be in prison."

"First things first, let me tell you how this works. I will place you in this harness, which flips you on your belly and tips your ass up. I won't remove your clothes, because as I said, I am not interested in sex or seeing your genitals. I will make a slit in your panties at your vaginal opening, so I can insert the turkey baster into you and squeeze in my semen. It worked on that bitch, so I can assume it will work with you. Don't worry. We have a few days before I can do this. I need to get a supply of sperm because we may have to try a few times before you become pregnant. I also don't want you to be so upset as you are now. It could affect you getting pregnant."

"You are out of your mind! Being that I am going to be a surrogate mother for your child, I will pick the time for this pregnancy," says Amanda.

"No, you won't, sweetheart," says Ron.

"If you want a healthy daughter, I highly suggest you abide by my wishes. You aren't dealing with a teenager here," says Amanda.

"We will see," says Ron as he leaves the basement.

# JULIA PIECES TOGETHER THE CASE

J ulia has come into the office for work and notices Amanda missing from her office. Amanda always gets to the office before she arrives.

---

"Richard and Bobbie, have you seen or heard from Amanda?" asks Julia.

"No, we haven't," says Bobbie.

"Betsy, what is it?" asks Julia.

"Chief, a girl from the Kroger Grocery, called and said one of our squad cars is parked in the parking lot and has been there overnight," says Betsy.

"Thank you, Betsy."

"Richard, please get over there to the grocery store on the way to the Sneer home. I believe the squad car Amanda was driving to get to the coroner's office is there. I am worried something has happened to Amanda, and I have a feeling we need to find out real fast," says Julia.

---

Richard pulls up to the squad car at Kroger's Grocery and sees Amanda's id in the car as well as some groceries. Just below the passenger door is a handkerchief. He picks it up and readily notices that it smells of Formaldehyde. He hurriedly walks into the supermarket and asks for a manager.

---

"Hello, I am Richard Peltz from the Harford Police Department, and the squad car out there is one of ours. Did anyone see the officer who was driving that car?"

"No, but there was a woman in here, about in her mid-twenties, purchasing protein drinks and a guy who was watching and following her around. It is the same guy I described to one of your female Officers. This guy usually shops once a month here, but lately, he has been in here weekly shopping for healthy foods such as fruits and vegetables. The day he was in here following that woman, he purchased six pregnancy test kits," says one of the clerks.

---

Richards thanks the clerk for her help and rushes out to his car.

---

"Julia, this is Richard. It appears Amanda was here. Her id is in the squad car and a bag of groceries. I found a handkerchief smelling of Formaldehyde on the ground outside her passenger door. The clerk in the store noted a woman matching Amanda's description being watched and followed by a man who has been purchasing healthy foods, and his recent purchase was for pregnancy test kits."

"Richard, did you get a description of this guy?" asks Julia.

"I sure did. Do you want me to wait here in case he comes back?"

"Yes, Richard, stay there until I call you back. Bobbie, we have to find Amanda! She is in danger! I am trying to piece my thoughts together," says Julia.

"Let's piece together what we know," says Bobbie.

"OK, we have a little girl who was hit and killed by the Sneer girl; we have Tom and his father; we have a dead girl from the pond who is the Sneer girl; the Sneer girl was raped resulting in pregnancy; we have a guy who buys healthy foods who doesn't usually purchase those types of groceries; he purchase pregnancy test kits; Amanda is kidnapped and probably in danger," says Julia.

"What are we missing, Julia?"

"The only thing we do have is a distraught father. The father of the little girl was probably angered and so distraught with the loss of his wife and then his daughter," says Julia.

"Do you think there is a connection to any of this?" asks Bobbie.

"Wait a minute! It may sound strange and bizarre. Suppose this father is so distraught to affect his mind to the point that he will do anything to get his daughter back. Suppose, in retribution, he kidnaps the person, the Sneer girl, who killed his daughter; rapes her to get her pregnant," says Julia.

"I think you are getting somewhere, but why would he kill the Sneer girl if he wanted her pregnant?" asks Bobbie.

"Wait a minute! He got her pregnant to birth a daughter for him. She died not by his hand, but by some mishap. He had to dispose of the dead girl, thus the pond. Oh, no! Oh, no!"

"What is it, Julia?"

"He has kidnapped Amanda to replace the Sneer girl to be the surrogate for his baby!"

"How convoluted is that?" asks Bobbie.

"We have to find Amanda now! Bobbie, get on the phone and get the Police Chief down in Kingsley, or someone, and get the name of the father who lost his daughter from the Sneer accident and his address. We don't have a moment to lose. I am on my way down there to get Richard and listen for your call. As soon as you call me with that information, you get in a car and rush down here to meet up with us. Use your lights! It is an emergency!"

# THE CUT THAT SAVES AMANDA'S VIRGINITY

Meanwhile, at Ron's home, he has taken his supply of semen out of the refrigerator and lets it set to warm to room temperature. He approaches Amanda.

---

"What are you going to do?" asks Amanda.

"It is time, sweetheart. Are you ready to carry my daughter?"

"If you release me, I will see to it that you get a chance to adopt a daughter," says Amanda.

"No, my daughter has to be my daughter with my genes."

"But she will not have your wife's genes. She will have mine. She will not be your daughter, like the one your wife conceived. Besides, you will lose custody of the baby I give birth to. She will be mine and not yours," says Amanda.

"She will be mine! Now cooperate with me while I connect you up to the saddle."

"I will not!" exclaims Amanda as she squirms.

"Fine, I will just drug you again."

"Then, you will need to wait for me to revive," says Amanda.

"It won't take as long as it will for me to fight you to get into the saddle."

---

Ron places the handkerchief across Amanda's mouth and nose as she slumps into sleep.

---

"Sweetheart, it took you a while to wake up, but now I finally have you in the saddle. Now, let me explain. As soon as my semen is at room temperature, I will start. Here, let me make the slit in your panties. Now don't move a muscle. I don't want to cut you down there."

---

Amanda contemplates on moving and getting cut. That might just stall him enough for her to get other ideas on how not to get impregnated. There is no time to think. As soon as Ron reaches for Amanda's panties and she feels his hand touch her labia through the cloth material, she jerks to the side as his scalpel slices into the side of her labia. The pain is immense.

---

"Damn it, woman! I told you not to move. Now I have your pussy bleeding. A temporary setback! I will just have to stop the bleeding."

"You aren't going to touch me anywhere down there! The deal was that you do not fondle me! You said that. I will take care of myself."

"Fine, but you are not getting out of this harness. I am not going through that again."

"Fine with me. Just leave me alone while the blood coagulates and stops," says Amanda.

"I suppose I could flip you on your back and unshackle one of your arms so you can doctor yourself."

"That would be very gentlemanly of you. With the locks on the remaining shackles, there would be no way I can escape," says Amanda.

"OK, but I am warning you. The other girl didn't survive her attempt to escape, and it wouldn't be so hard for me to do away with you seeing you are not carrying my child yet."

"Hand that salve over to me," says Amanda.

"It isn't salve. It is a vaginal lubricant in case you were dry down there."

"Don't you know about the medicinal properties of that lubricant!" exclaims Amanda.

"OK, here you go."

"Now leave me! You are not going to watch me doctor, my genitals."

"OK, I will be upstairs. In about thirty minutes, I will be down to administer the semen, so you better hope you are better down there."

---

Amanda spreads the lubricant on her wrists and tests whether she can slide her hands out of the shackles. After a couple of tries, success comes to her as her hands are free. She can push the handcuffs on her wrists again, so Ron doesn't see her loose. She is sure she can slip them back off. Amanda performs another dry run in removing the shackles, and while her hands are free, she sees the turkey baster lying on the table next to her. It is already filled with semen, and she squirms as she picks it up and hides it in her hand after she slides back into the shackles.

Amanda hears Ron approach the stairway to the basement.

"OK, sweetheart, time is up to whether your bleeding has stopped or not."

"It has stopped enough," says Amanda.

"I am going to flip you over on your belly again. Oh, hell, what did I do with that turkey baster? Hold on. I need to find where I put that thing before I can flip you."

"I think you laid it over here," says Amanda.

Ron moves over towards Amanda and starts to look just as she sits up and grabs the baster with her free hand from behind her back and shoves it into his mouth until he gags, and she then squeezes the bulb.

# RONALD TIER HAS LOST HIS DAUGHTER FOREVER

As soon as Amanda finishes squeezing the bulb, Julia, Bobbie, and Richard come rushing down the stairway to the basement.

---

"Freeze, Ronald Tier! Stop right there!" exclaims Julia.

Ron coughs the baster out of his mouth, and his semen is running out between his lips.

Richard quickly puts handcuffs on Ron as Bobbie holds her gun to his head.

"You have the right to remain silent. Anything you say can and will be held against you in a court of law," says Richard.

"Amanda are you OK?" asks Julia.

"Yes, help me get the shackles off my legs and get me out of this harness."

"Give me the keys to the shackles, Mr. Tier! Amanda, you are bleeding. Did he…"

"No, Julia, he did not get a chance to shove that turkey baster into me to impregnate me, which was his intent."

"My daughter…she is gone..my daughter is dead," says Ron weeping.

"Richard, take Mr. Tier to the car. Bobbie and I will be up to join you after we administer to Amanda. You are bleeding from your vagina. Do you mind if I pull down your panties enough to see how badly hurt you are?" asks Julia

"No go ahead," says Amanda.

"Looks like he cut your labia," says Bobbie.

"Yes, I figured the only way to stall him further was to move when he was trying to slit my panties to insert the turkey baster. When he cut me, it hurt like hell, but it bought me thirty minutes and a method to get loose enough to shove that baster down his throat. It is a good thing you came when you did because I think I would have continued to shove that thing down his throat until he choked to death," says Amanda.

"Well, at least he didn't penetrate you with his penis or the turkey baster," says Bobbie.

"Yeah, I am not ready to have a baby. My baby will be made by a husband I love dearly and me," says Amanda.

"You go, girl!" exclaims Bobbie.

"How did you know where to find me?"

"Amanda, it was because of Julia's hunches," says Bobbie.

"Wait a minute, ladies, it was a cooperative effort. The important thing is you are OK, and I still have a Forensics Specialist on my team and a damn good one, too," says Julia.

"Julia, I will take Amanda to the ER while you travel back to the office with Richard. As soon as Amanda is doctored, we will return and join you," says Bobbie.

"Great! Amanda, it is so good to see you again! I was worried about you. You are part of our family here," says Julia.

"Thank you, Julia," says Amanda.

Julia and Richard stop at the Police Department in Kingsley to deliver Ron to them and document the specifics of the case which were not earlier transmitted to them.

On the way back to the Harford Police Department, Julia and Richard continue to discuss the case.

———

"Julia, why is it that we get such bazaar and strange cases?" asks Richard.

"Richard, I don't think that these cases are so strange; it has all to do to where our society is going. People are getting weirder and more corrupted each year that passes."

———

Julia and Richard pull into the Harford Police Department parking lot and walk exhaustingly to the entrance. As soon as Julia enters the reception area, Betsy runs up to her.

———

"Julia, I just received a phone call from a Mrs. Samuels. She says her husband has been missing for two days and would like our help in finding him."

"Oh, Betsy, not another missing persons. I am so tired and not ready for another missing persons."

"I am so sorry, Julia. I did tell her to wait until we responded when you returned."

"That's OK Betsy, I will look into it as soon as I get the reports finished for the Sneer case."

"Julia, do you think this missing persons will be another bizarre matter?" asks Richard.

"Heaven knows, Richard. You have had a big day today, and as soon as Bobbie and Amanda return, take your wife home. I can do what needs to be done. Go and enjoy your little ones."

"OK, Julia, I will be in bright and early tomorrow morning to tackle this missing person's case," says Richard.

# ABOUT THE AUTHOR

James Roberts, an emerging author of fictional Crime Thrillers, delivers to his readers the realization of twisted feelings, minds, and actions as well as true-to-life situations leading to criminal activities that are sometimes hard to fathom.

This is James Robert's fourth book.

www.ingramcontent.com/pod-product-compliance
Lightning Source LLC
Chambersburg PA
CBHW020141150626
46552CB00021B/1209